So Many Cats!

So Many Cats!

by Beatrice Schenk de Regniers

Illustrated by Ellen Weiss

Clarion Books

TICKNOR & FIELDS: A HOUGHTON MIFFLIN COMPANY

New York

Clarion Books
Ticknor & Fields, a Houghton Mifflin Company
Text copyright © 1985 by Beatrice Schenk de Regniers
Illustrations copyright © 1985 by Ellen Weiss

Printed in the U.S.A.

Library of Congress Cataloging in Publication Data
de Regniers, Beatrice Schenk.
So many cats!
Summary: Counting verses explain how a family ended
up with a dozen cats.
1. Children's stories, American. [1. Cats—Fiction.
2. Counting.   3. Stories in rhyme] I. Weiss, Ellen, ill.
II. Title
PZ8.3.D443Sn 1985   [E]   85-3739
ISBN 0-89919-322-6

H 10 9 8 7 6 5 4 3 2 1

For Olivia and Marianne

—B.deR.

To my grandmother, Amelia,
with love

—E.W.

We have sister cats
and brother cats,
father cats
and mother cats.
How come we have a dozen cats?
Here's how:

We had a cat—
an Only Cat.
She was a sad
and lonely cat.

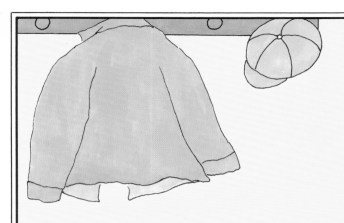

So when a very hungry cat
came making a great din,
meowing, mewing,
scratching at our door,
we thought
this could be the very cat
to make our cat a happy cat,
and so we let her in —

little knowing we were getting more
than we had
bargained
for.

Next morning,
we found that now this other cat
had turned into a mother cat.
So
instead of two cats
we
had
four!
No! . . . FIVE!!

Three little kittens
very much alive:
    Fluffy and *Muffy* and *Smoke*,

plus *Tammy,* their mammy,
and *Poke*—Poke,
once our Only—
now no longer lonely—
Cat.

Then,
a neighbor moving to another city
came to chat, she said,
and say goodbye.
She'd brought her cat. She said
that her cat's name was *Kitty.*
Then she began to cry.

The cat was good as gold, she said.
But the cat was very old. She said
she couldn't take the cat along.
Then, about to cry again,
she quickly said goodbye again,
and left.
We said, "So long."

Then we counted our cats to see
how many cats we had now:
    a very old cat named *Kitty*,
    Fluffy and *Muffy* and *Smoke*,
    plus *Tammy*, their mammy,
    and *Poke*.
Did you count six? So did we.
That's not too bad now.

Last month, my little brother, Matt,
brought home such an ugly cat!
A chewed-up ear;
one eye blind.
He was so dear,
we didn't mind

his looks.
But it would be a pity
if he knew that he was ugly,
so we named him *"Pretty."*

My sister, Lee,
that very day
took a bus ride
all the way
into the city.

And that night
my sister, Lee,
came home with—
not *one* cat,
but three!

Three
frumpy, fleasy,
skinny, sleazy
city cats.

Now, of course,
they would be getting
lots of loving, petting,
feeding.
That was all
those cats were needing
to change from skinny city cats
into three plump and pretty cats.

Have I named nine cats or ten?
I think we'd better count cats again.

There are my sister's cats:
  Jenny and *Penny* and *Bloke*;
  Matt's ugly cat named *Pretty*;
  a very old cat named *Kitty*;
  Fluffy, Muffy, and *Smoke*,
  plus *Tammy*, their mammy,
  and *Poke*.

Is that ten?
You're sure?
Well then,
there must be more — two more —
cats not yet accounted for.
Here they are!
They followed me home from the grocery store.
Dawn and *Night.*
Night's black.
Dawn's white.

Do you think we could
count cats again?
What! Again?
Yes. I think we should
count cats again—
just once more
as we did before
and then we're through for good.

All right!
There's
    Dawn.
There's
    Night.
There are my sister's cats,
    Jenny and *Penny* and *Bloke;*
    Matt's ugly cat named *Pretty;*
    a very old cat named *Kitty;*
    Fluffy, Muffy, and *Smoke,*
    plus *Tammy,* their mammy,
    and *Poke*—Poke,
    once our Only—
    now no longer lonely—
Cat.

Twelve cats.
That's enough cats.
I adore cats.
But I don't want more cats.
Is that clear?

What's that I hear?
A strange meow—
don't look now—
outside the window . . .

Oh!
What a dear
little cat!